HARI AND HIS
ELECTRIC FEET

HARI AND HIS ELECTRIC FEET

ALEXANDER McCALL SMITH

With illustrations by
Sam Usher

Conkers

First published in 2018 in Great Britain by
Barrington Stoke Ltd
18 Walker Street, Edinburgh, EH3 7LP

www.barringtonstoke.co.uk

Text © 2018 Alexander McCall Smith
Illustrations © 2018 Sam Usher

A CIP catalogue record for this book is available
from the British Library upon request

ISBN: 978-1-78112-755-1

Printed in Great Britain by Clays Ltd, St Ives plc

For Harry and Ruaridh

Contents

1. Hari   1

2. At Mr Ram's place   12

3. A magic gift   24

4. Could we have a show?   35

5. Everybody started dancing   49

6. Meeting Laxy and Gav   59

7. The thieves learn a lesson   71

8. No admission   83

9. A very rowdy meeting   97

10. World peace now!   109

CHAPTER ONE

Hari

This is the story of a boy who could dance. Lots of boys can dance, but there was something special about the way Hari danced. It was so special, in fact, that it changed everything for Hari – and for other people too. It was so special that when I heard about it, I decided that I should write the whole story down. And here it is – the story of Hari exactly as it happened.

Hari lived in a city in India. This city was

not the biggest city in the country – there are some very large cities in India – but it was still big enough. Nobody knows exactly how many people lived in this city, as it had been some time since they had all been counted. But just about everybody agreed that there were over one million people who made their home there. One million people is a lot of people – try to imagine them all lined up. If you started walking along the line early in the morning, just as the sun came up, you'd still be walking at the end of the day, when the sun went down and the birds all flew off to their beds in the trees.

Here is a picture of Hari. He was twelve at the time of our story and you will see that he has a friendly smile. People like boys who smile, and Hari was popular because he always smiled

at others when he spoke to them. They also liked

him because he was kind. Hari did things for

other people, even when they did not ask him to.

Most people liked that. He would also share the things he had. They liked that very much indeed.

Hari lived with his older sister, Amala, and his aunt. His parents did not live with them because there was no work for them in that city. They lived a long way away, in the countryside, in the hills of a place called Assam, where they grow a lot of tea. Their job was to pick and prepare the tea in a large tea garden owned by a wealthy man, a mean and unhappy person who thought only of money. It was not well-paid work, and their life was a hard one. That was why the aunt had offered to take the children.

"If they live with me," she said, "then that will mean there are two fewer mouths for you to feed."

Their parents knew that this was true. At

the same time, they did not want to say goodbye to their children, and it was a sad day for them when they waved the two children off at the beginning of their train journey to their new home. They hoped that one day the family would be reunited, but they also knew that this might never happen.

Both children tried to be brave.

"We'll see them again next year," Amala said, as the train snaked its way out of the railway station. "Or maybe the year after that."

"That won't be the same as seeing them every day," Hari muttered, fighting back his tears.

"No," said his sister. "But I'm sure you'll be happy enough living in a city. Just think of all the things there are to do in a big place like that."

She was right about that, of course. There were many new and exciting things to do in the city, but you had to have a bit of money to do most of them. Unfortunately, Hari and his sister were poor, as was their aunt.

"I'm sorry that there won't be much spare money," she said to her nephew and niece. "But if we all work hard we shall get by all right."

The work that the aunt did had to do with clothes. She was a seamstress and she had a sewing machine that she worked by treading on a pedal beneath it. This was an old-fashioned way of sewing, but at least it did not use any electricity and the aunt was skilled at making the best of what she had in life.

Amala and Hari soon found out what work they were expected to do. Amala was to assist her aunt with dress-making and with repairs to people's clothes. She also sometimes helped a woman who lived down the street to look after her young daughter, who was three years old, and her even younger son, who was barely one. That could be hard work, too, as children that small can be very demanding.

Hari's job was to deliver food for a man who ran a nearby take-away restaurant. At noon each day, when school stopped for lunch, Hari would pick up all the lunch boxes that had been prepared for the customers. These were called *tiffin boxes* and they contained the tasty curries and breads that the chef had cooked that morning. People who worked in offices would eat their lunch from their tiffin boxes, and then later in the afternoon Hari would call to collect the empty boxes. He would wash these once he got back to the restaurant and stack them up ready for the next day. That was his main job.

But Hari also had another job, which was to make sweets. For as long as he could remember he had been good at making special Indian sweets, and the aunt had encouraged him to do this when he went to live with her.

"I'll start you off with the ingredients," she said. "You make the sweets and then you can sell plates of them from outside our door. People will love them." She paused. "And once you've paid me back for the ingredients, you can keep the rest of the money."

Hari was very pleased with this arrangement, and he soon became quite well known to the people who walked to work along the street on which the aunt lived.

"That boy's sweets are really delicious," people said. "They are so tasty that we can't resist them!"

With the small amount of money that he earned from selling his sweets, Hari was able to treat himself to a seat at the local cinema every Saturday afternoon. He loved the films shown there – the great adventures made by the film studios in Mumbai. He loved everything that happened in these films – the horse-riding, the treasure-hunting, the thrilling car chases and, of course, the dancing. Hari loved to watch people dancing.

"I like to watch dancing even more than I like to make and eat sweets," he said to his sister.

Amala looked at him with surprise. "Are you sure?" she asked.

Hari nodded. "Completely sure," he answered. "One hundred per cent."

"If you like dancing so much," Amala said, "then why have I never seen you dance? Why don't you dance yourself?"

Hari thought about this for a few moments. "Maybe I shall," he said. "One day."

CHAPTER TWO

At Mr Ram's place

One of the people to whom Hari delivered a tiffin
box every lunch time was called Mr Ram.

Mr Ram was an old man who lived at the
end of Hari's street, in a house with a red roof.
This house looked small from the outside, but had
a lot of room inside. From the front door, there
led a long, narrow corridor that ended in a room
at the back, overlooking the yard. That is where
Mr Ram sat, watching the birds in his garden

and reading one of the many
books from the shelves that
lined the walls. Because he fed
the birds, Mr Ram's room was
always filled with bird song. To
Hari it seemed that these birds
were thanking Mr Ram for the seed he left out for
them and for the fact that he did not allow any
cats to come into his garden. Birds are always
very grateful for that.

Hari did not have to knock. Carrying the
blue tiffin box carefully, so as not to spill any
of the delicious sauces and gravies it contained,
Hari would make his way along the long corridor
and call out to Mr Ram just before he entered the
room.

"*Tiffin wallah!*" he would shout.

And from within the room, Mr Ram would call out, "Come right in, Hari!"

Hari could not stay for long, as he had other deliveries to make, but he always enjoyed a chat with Mr Ram. Sometimes it was about the food that the restaurant had chosen for him that day – at other times it was about things that had been reported in the papers. Mr Ram liked to read the newspaper, and he would tell Hari about the day's main stories.

"Another train has come off the rails," he might say, with a shake of his head. "It's about time they fixed the railway lines, don't you think, Hari?"

Or he might say, "The weather forecast says it will rain tomorrow. I think they're right, you know."

Hari found that he agreed with most of the things that Mr Ram said, as the old man was very wise. *He has seen a lot in his lifetime,* Hari thought, although he had never found out exactly what Mr Ram's job had been. He had never asked him directly, although now and then Mr Ram

would make some remark about having worked with famous people. But he never said much more than that, and Hari somehow knew that one day he would tell him – in his own good time.

Hari often used to take a small parcel of home-made sweets to Mr Ram. These he made for him as a gift, and he would not accept any money for them. Hari knew that Mr Ram had a sweet tooth, and particularly liked a special sort of coconut sweet that Hari made.

"I have eaten *barfi* all my life, but I have never tasted anything quite as delicious as this," Mr Ram said, as he took one of the sticky confections out of the packet. "Oh, Hari, you must be one of the best sweet-makers in all India."

Hari laughed at this. He knew his sweets were good – but surely not *that* good.

Mr Ram's house was usually Hari's last call on his lunchtime rounds. After that, he had a bit of spare time in which he could do anything he liked, before he had to go home to carry out any chores his aunt had for him. Sometimes he spent this spare time with one or two of his close friends, watching buses load up at the nearby bus station, or playing cricket in a dusty little park

not far away. On other occasions, he would go to
the market to get the ingredients needed for his
next batch of sweets. He enjoyed that, as he liked
to barter with the stall-keepers, hoping to buy his
milk and spices, coconut and sugar at the lowest
possible price.

On that day, though, Hari's attention was
caught by an unusual sight. A few blocks away
from their house, at the entrance to a street of
old houses, two policemen were placing a road
block so that no cars could enter the street.

Hari knew one of the policemen slightly. He
had sometimes bought a bag or
two of his sweets, and Hari
remembered that he had a

particular fondness for any sweets with pineapple in them.

"Hey, Mr Pineapple," Hari called out. "What's going on?"

The policeman looked at him and smiled. He did not seem to mind being called Mr Pineapple, and he gave Hari a cheerful wave.

"So it's you, Mr Sweet-Maker," the policeman called back. "Somebody's making a film."

Hari crossed the street to join them. 'What sort of film?" he asked.

The policeman shrugged. "Who knows? All we were told to do is to block off this street so that they can bring in their film trucks."

"They need a mountain of equipment to make a film," said the other policeman. "You or I could do it with far less."

Hari looked down the street. "Am I allowed to walk down there?" he asked.

The first policeman thought for a moment. "Well, all they told us was to stop any traffic, so I think you could. But make sure you don't get in their way."

Hari thanked Mr Pineapple and began to walk down the street. It seemed a bit quiet, without the usual traffic, but he soon came upon a line of large parked trucks, surrounded by a general bustle of people. As he approached, he saw that equipment was being unloaded from one of the trucks and carried further down the street where carpenters were busy making something large.

"Hey, you," said a voice suddenly. "Don't just stand there – get moving."

It was clear to Hari that the man who gave him this order thought that he was one of the employees who were working hard at unloading equipment.

"Come on," the man urged again. "You're not being paid to stand about."

Hari was about to explain that he was just a passer-by when he stopped himself. Why should he not carry things for these film people? He had never seen a film set before and he might never get another chance to  see one. So, without further ado, he ran across to one of the trucks and picked up a large coil of electric wire. Then he followed one of the other carriers and took it to the place where the carpenters had created a film set in the middle of the street.

"Put that over there," said a man with a clipboard. "Then go and get the rest."

Hari did as he was told, and for the next hour he carried equipment between the trucks and the stage. When everything was in place, he and the other carriers – all of whom were a bit older than he was – were given a mug of tea and a thick slice of cake.

"You people," said the man with the clipboard, "may watch the action, as long as you don't make a noise. We'll need you again to put the equipment away for the night."

Hari squatted down on the pavement and watched as the great cameras started to film what was happening on the set. It was fascinating, and time passed very quickly. And then it happened. A set of speakers started to belt out a catchy dance tune. This was the signal to the actors to break out into one of the most energetic dances Hari had ever seen.

He could not take his eyes off the scene. *If only I could dance like that*, thought Hari.

CHAPTER THREE

A magic gift

Hari arrived home later than usual.

"Where have you been all afternoon?" asked his aunt in a rather cross tone. "I've had to send your sister, rather than you, to deliver some cloth."

"Sorry, Aunty," Hari said. "I was watching a film being made."

He told his aunt about how he had been mistaken for a member of the crew, and she laughed and seemed to become less cross.

"Did they pay you, Mr Film Director?"

Hari shook his head. "That didn't matter, though. I loved every minute of it."

"Films!" his aunt snorted. "They don't show the world the way it really is. All that music and dancing – that's not what the world is really about."

Hari did not say anything. He was thinking of the dance steps he had seen and he had decided that after he had finished talking to his aunt, he would go out into the yard at the back and practise some of them. He had never danced before, but he was sure that he would be able to imitate the dancers on the film set. It did not look too difficult, after all, and if they could do it he saw no reason why he could not.

Once his aunt had returned to her

work-room, Hari went out into the yard and looked about him. He was on his own, apart from a couple of chickens and the neighbours' dog, which liked to lie under the small tree in the centre of the yard. The chickens did not seem to mind the dog, as they knew that he was far too old to have the energy to get up and chase them. So they pecked about in the dirt while the dog snored away under his tree.

Hari did not have a player for the music the

dancers had danced to,

and so he had to hum it himself.

But that was no problem, as he had a good

memory for tunes and could remember the notes

quite easily. Now he started to hum, and as he

did so, he took the first hesitant steps of one of

the dances he had seen a few hours earlier.

The effect was extraordinary. There are

some people who have a gift of doing something

perfectly the very first time they do it, and

Hari was one of these – at least when it came to

dancing. He had never really done anything about

it, but he had a natural sense of rhythm and,

in addition to that, he could move with all the sleekness of a panther.

No sooner had Hari began than he was dancing superbly, and as he did so something very strange happened. The chickens stopped their pecking at the ground and stared at Hari with that odd sense of puzzlement that you often see in chickens. Then, clucking and crowing as if they were singing along to the music, they began to dance. And they danced in perfect time, imitating, in their chicken-like way, every step that Hari took.

That was strange enough, but it does not end there. The neighbours' dog, having opened one eye to observe Hari, now opened both. Then the dog sat bolt upright, as if he recognised the tune that Hari was humming. He was still for a few moments before he leaped to his feet and also began to dance – swaying from side to side in exactly the same way as Hari was doing.

When Hari stopped dancing for a moment, then the chickens and the dog stopped as well. They looked about them, feeling a bit foolish,

perhaps, and wondering what had happened to them. But when Hari started to dance again, this time trying out a few new steps he had invented himself, the chickens and the dog started again.

Hari thought it tremendous fun. And when one of his friends popped his head over the fence to see what was going on, he too was caught up in the magic.

"What are you doing, Hari?" the friend asked.

Hari looked up and smiled. "Just dancing," he answered.

And with that the friend wriggled his way through the fence and was soon dancing alongside Hari, following his steps exactly, just as if the two of them were puppets, dangling on strings controlled by the hand of some hidden puppeteer.

"This is great," said the friend when at last they stopped. "Where did you learn to do this, Hari?"

Hari shrugged. "I'm not sure," he replied. "I saw some film people dancing – I must have picked it up from them."

"But you made those chickens and that old dog dance too," said the friend. "And me as well. I don't know why, but I just felt I had to join in."

Hari had no idea why his dancing seemed to have this effect. But it was time now for him to go inside and help his aunt prepare the evening meal, so he said goodbye to his

friend and promised that they could dance again some other time. The chickens went back to being ordinary chickens again,

31

but somehow they seemed more pleased with themselves, as if they had just done something rather important and had made their yard, and the dust in which they pecked, a better place.

*

The following day, Hari went back to the street where the film crew had been working. They were still there, and they seemed to be happy enough to give him a few chores to perform. It was a hot day and Hari's job was to take bottles of water to the actors and dancers during their breaks. He was kept busy, but not so busy that he could not watch what was going on, and by the end of the afternoon, when the crew packed up and prepared to go home, Hari had learned a number of new dance routines.

It was while he was trying these out, in a quiet corner of the set, that two of the dancers came across him. They watched him for a few moments, surprised to find a boy who could dance so well, and then, once again, a very strange thing happened. The two dancers suddenly joined in, twirling and whirling around Hari, following his every step.

When he stopped, the dancers looked at one another in astonishment.

"What happened there?" asked one.

"I don't know," said the other. "I just suddenly felt I had to dance. It was as if some unseen force was making me do it."

They both stared at Hari. Then one said, "We don't know who you are. We thought you were just the boy who brought us bottles of water."

Hari nodded politely. "I'm called Hari," he said. "And I'm just that boy."

Both the dancers smiled. "You may be just a boy," said one, "but you are a boy with some sort of magic gift. You do know that, don't you?"

Hari was unsure what to say. He was as surprised as they were about this strange power he had, and he was not sure where it would lead.

Well, it was going to lead to some quite unexpected adventures, and of course Hari had no idea what these would be.

34

CHAPTER FOUR

Could we have a show?

The film people packed up and left. They had finished what they were doing, and the street in which they had been filming now returned to normal. Hari felt disappointed, as he had enjoyed the excitement of the set and his small, unpaid job on its fringes, but he soon got back to his ordinary life. His aunt had received an order for twenty waiters' uniforms, and this kept her and Amala so busy that they had no time for much

else. It was left to Hari to go to the shops, buy the food, and even do quite a bit of the preparation of the evening meal. He peeled potatoes, shelled peas, and crushed the spices that would go into his aunt's dishes. Then he washed fruit and chopped up mangos for the mango *lassi* that was his favourite drink. After that, he would sweep the veranda and polish the stone floor of the bathroom. There was always something to do in their house. It may have been small, and it may have been in need of a coat of paint, but it was their home and they all took pride in keeping it in good order.

Alongside all this, Hari had to deliver his tiffin boxes, including the one that he took to Mr Ram. It was when he delivered the next day that Mr Ram asked him a question.

"I hear they've been making a film nearby," he remarked. "Did you see them, by any chance, Hari?"

Hari told Mr Ram about how he had been given a job on the set. Mr Ram listened with interest and then asked Hari whether there had been any dancing.

"Yes, there was dancing," replied Hari. "There was a lot of dancing."

Mr Ram smiled as he looked up at the ceiling. It seemed as if he was remembering something from a long time ago.

"I used to be able to dance," he said. "In fact, although I say it myself ..." He broke off. It was as if he were embarrassed about what he was about to say.

Hari waited, but Mr Ram seemed lost in thought. Eventually Hari spoke. "What sort of dancing?" he asked.

Mr Ram's gaze came down from the ceiling. "If I tell you," he said, "will you promise not to tell anyone?"

Hari gave his word. He was good at keeping secrets.

"It was a long time ago," began Mr Ram. "I used to be younger than I am today, you know."

Hari knew that this was one of Mr Ram's jokes, and he laughed. Everybody in the world could say that, he realised.

"In those days I lived in Mumbai," Mr Ram went on. "That's where they have the big film studios. You know how they call it Bollywood." Mr Ram knew Hari loved to watch films.

Hari's eyes widened. "Were you a Bollywood star, Mr Ram?"

"Good gracious, no!" answered Mr Ram. "Nothing that grand. But I can say that I *made* one or two film stars in my time."

Hari was puzzled, but he did not have to wait long for an explanation.

"You see," said Mr Ram, "I had a dance

studio. I used to teach actors how to dance. Other people came too – those who simply wanted to learn how to do ballroom dancing or whatever."

Hari listened in rapt attention as Mr Ram told the rest of the story. He had been well-known, he said, and people came to his studio from far and wide. Some of them could not dance very well, even after a full course of lessons, and had to accept they would never dance in a movie, but others ... Mr Ram mentioned the names of one or two famous film stars whom he had taught to dance. Hari was impressed, as he had seen these people in the movies.

"You taught *him* to dance?" asked Hari, mentioning the name of one very famous Bollywood star.

Mr Ram nodded modestly. "Yes," he said.

"You know, he was very clumsy when he first came to me. I used to call him Mr Two-Left-Feet. But then after a few lessons he became one of the best dancers I've ever seen."

Now Mr Ram became silent, and it seemed to Hari that the old man was feeling sad about something.

"Did something happen?" asked Hari.

Mr Ram nodded. "My studio burned down in a fire," he said. "I think it was started by a rival. There was another dance studio, you see, that wanted the business. They paid some scallywag to burn my studio down one night. Fortunately, nobody was hurt, but the building, which was my pride and joy, was reduced to a pile of ashes. That was all that was left of my life's work."

Hari felt sorry for the old man. He could

imagine what it was like to lose everything.

"Did the police catch the person who did it?" he asked.

"Sadly, no," said Mr Ram. "We were unable to prove anything. The villains got away with it."

"And you?" asked Hari. "Did you get another place?"

"No," said Mr Ram. "I had saved a bit of money, I'm happy to say, and I decided to come and live here. I was born in this town, you see. This house used to belong to my parents and it was now mine. So I came back."

Hari said nothing as he thought about this tale. He had always liked Mr Ram, and it made him sad to hear of the loss that the old man had

suffered. It seemed to him that the world could

be very unfair at times – bad things happened

and those who made them happen sometimes

went unpunished. If he had anything to do with it, things would be different.

"But I don't want to talk about my troubles," Mr Ram said. "What's past is past. Tell me more about the dancing you saw on that film set."

Hari described what he had witnessed, but then offered to show Mr Ram what he had learned.

"A good idea," said Mr Ram. "Should I play some music?"

Hari waited while Mr Ram put a record on his ancient record player. Then, at full volume, the sound of a famous dance tune filled the room.

Hari began to dance. In his mind, he was no longer in Mr Ram's living room, but somewhere else altogether, in a great hall with marble floors and shining lights. And the steps he had seen came back to him as easily and naturally as if he had practised them for days and days.

Mr Ram watched. At first he simply looked surprised, but, as Hari got into his dance, his eyes began to shine. Then, rising to his feet, he began to dance too. It was just as it had been with the chickens and the dog. It was no different from the way it had been with Hari's friend and with the

dancers who had spoken to Hari on the film set. Hari made Mr Ram dance as he had not danced for years and years.

When the music came to an end, Mr Ram sat down and stared at Hari. He wiped his forehead with a handkerchief.

"I have never seen anything like it in my

life," he said, his voice cracked with emotion. "You're an infectious dancer, Hari. I've never come across that before. Never."

Hari looked modestly at the floor. He did not intend to get people dancing – it just seemed to happen. He thought about what Mr Ram had said. He had called him an infectious dancer. Hari knew what infectious meant – something was infectious if it could be passed on to somebody else – like a cold. Was that what his special gift was – the ability to pass on the desire to dance?

Mr Ram had been having his own thoughts. "Could we have a little show?" he asked. "Nothing big – just for the neighbours in the street."

"With me dancing?" asked Hari.

"Yes," said Mr Ram. "I'm sure other people would like to see it." He paused. "I don't want to press you to say yes, Hari, but if you have an unusual gift it's good to share it with the world." He paused again. "And you do have that gift, you know."

Hari knew that he should say yes to what Mr Ram asked. And that is what he said, going on to ask, "When do you want to do this, Mr Ram?"

"Tomorrow," said Mr Ram, without delay. "Some things are too important to wait, and this is one of them."

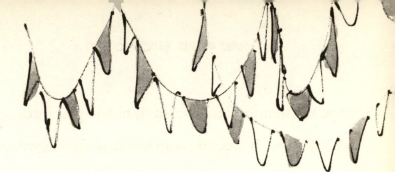

CHAPTER FIVE

Everybody started dancing

Mr Ram put out the word to neighbours that there would be a concert in the street the next day and it would be free. He did not tell them what the main attraction of the concert would be.

"That will be a surprise," he said. "If you want to know who the star of the show will be, then you'll have to come along. No tickets required – just turn up."

And they did turn up – in larger numbers

than Mr Ram had expected, but because the concert was being held in the open street, there was room for everybody.

The concert took place in the early evening, when it was still light, but at a time when the sun was less fierce. Hari arrived early, as Mr Ram had asked him to do, and saw that Mr Ram had bedecked a section of the pavement with flags. It was there that he was going to dance.

The crowds began to arrive, including Hari's aunt and Amala.

"What is all this about a show?" asked Amala. "And who's going to be in it?"

Hari swallowed hard. "Well, it's going to be me."

Amala looked at him in disbelief. "You?" she said. "You're going to be in a show?"

The aunt, of course, was more encouraging. "I always thought that Hari had talent," she said. "I've always thought that ..." She hesitated. "But what are you actually going to do?"

"I'm going to dance," said Hari.

"You?" Amala sneered. "Since when have you been able to dance?"

"I started a few days ago," muttered Hari.

He knew that this sounded very strange – to put on a public show when you had only just started to dance, but it was too late to change his mind now.

"He'll do it very well," the aunt said. "Good luck, Hari."

Mr Ram had found a special outfit for Hari. This was made up of a smart pair of trousers, a bright red shirt, and a pair of shiny black shoes.

"Your Bollywood outfit," he said as he handed the bundle to Hari. "The owner of that shop over there says you can go and get changed inside."

When Hari reappeared in his dancing clothes, the crowd was already assembled. Mr Ram had borrowed a loudspeaker and he now announced to the audience that the show would begin.

"We are most fortunate to have in this town one of the best young dancers in the country," he said. "And today we're going to see him in action."

The crowd applauded politely as Mr Ram led Harry to the makeshift stage. Then the music started and Hari began to dance. He tried not to look at the crowd, as he was worried that this would put him off his step. But he need not have worried – the moment he took his first step he felt a strange, almost electric energy take hold of him. After that, he did not care who was watching him – the dance took over. He

jumped, twisting and turning in the air. He glided forwards, backwards and sideways. His feet, in their shiny black shoes, moved so quickly that at times they were just a blur.

Mr Ram watched, and smiled as he saw what now began to happen. At first, people in the audience simply tapped their feet. Then, one by one, they began to take a few steps themselves. After that, it was not long before the whole audience – every man and woman, every boy and girl – was dancing in time with the music and with Hari's amazing steps.

At the end of the street, two policemen who had been passing by came to see what was going

on. When they reached the edge of the crowd, they too began to dance, throwing their caps in the air, caught up in the excitement of it all. Nobody there knew exactly why they were dancing – they all just felt the urge to dance alongside Hari.

Only two people were standing still. One was Mr Ram. He was in charge of the music, but he was also very carefully watching what was happening.

"It's a miracle," he muttered to himself. "It's little short of a miracle."

The other person who was not dancing was a tall boy standing in the shade of a shop veranda. He was following what was going on with keen interest, although he was keeping himself back in the shadows. After a while, he slipped away, disappearing down a side street. Nobody paid any attention to him. Nobody saw him go.

Like everybody else there, Hari had been enjoying himself. When he stopped, and the applause of the audience burst out, he was surrounded by people wanting to shake his hand, pat him on the back,  or tell him how much they liked his dancing. Everybody was smiling – not only had dancing broken out, but friendship too.

"You see," Mr Ram whispered in Hari's ear. "You see what a great gift you have? You've made all these people smile. You've made them hug one another. You've made them feel good about the world."

Hari smiled. He was pleased that the show had been a success. He was not to know, of course, what would happen the very next day.

CHAPTER SIX

Meeting Laxy and Gav

It happened at lunchtime, while Hari was delivering tiffin boxes. He had completed his main delivery and had also dropped off Mr Ram's lunch. Mr Ram had been pleased to see him and they had spent some time talking about the show. Everybody, said Mr Ram, agreed that it had been a great success.

Now Hari was walking home from Mr Ram's house when he heard a voice behind him.

"You're Hari, aren't you?"

Hari turned around. Behind him there were two boys of about his own age. The one who had

spoken was a bit taller than the other. Both were dressed in smart new jeans. Both were smiling.

"Yes," said Hari. "That's me."

The taller boy took a step forward and placed a friendly arm around Hari's shoulder. "You were great yesterday," he said. "We saw you, didn't we, Gav?"

The other boy, Gav, nodded. "We were there when you made everybody dance. It was terrific."

The taller boy now introduced himself. "I'm Laxy," he said. He took his arm from Hari's shoulder and offered him his hand to shake. Hari shook it.

"Do you like money?" asked Laxy.

Hari was surprised by the question. Most people liked money because they needed it. It did not seem like a very sensible thing to ask.

"Well?" Laxy pressed when Hari was slow to reply. "Do you?"

"I suppose so," said Hari. "Who doesn't?"

His own question was left unanswered. Now Laxy lowered his voice. "Gav and I know a great way of getting money," he said. "Would you like to see?"

Hari frowned. He was not sure about Gav and Laxy. They seemed friendly enough, but there was something about them that made him feel uneasy.

"Oh, we aren't asking you to go off anywhere," said Gav. "You only have to come with us to the market."

The market was just around the corner, and it was a place that Hari knew well. There could be no harm, he thought, in seeing how they made money in the market. Perhaps they had a stall there. Perhaps he would be able to sell the sweets he made at their stall and find more customers that way.

Hari thought of the things he could do with a bit more money. He had always wanted a bicycle, and if he made a bit more money he could save up and buy one. And then his aunt's birthday was coming up and he could buy her a bigger present if he could afford it. He knew she would be pleased because she always thought of others first and never treated herself to anything.

"Well?" asked Gav. "Do you want to come with us?"

Hari decided to say yes. These two boys might become good friends – you never knew – and he had remembered now that he had promised to pick up some spices from the market for his aunt. Since he had to go there anyway, he might as well see what these two had to show him.

It was only a few streets away and they reached it within minutes. It was a busy time in the market, with a lot of people using their lunch break to do some shopping. All the stalls were busy, the stall-holders engaged in frenzied bargaining with customers, trying to agree on a price, or trying to get the best available onions, or batteries, or any of the thousand and one things on offer.

As they stood at the end of a line of stalls, Laxy turned to Hari and said, "Will you do one of your dances?"

Hari raised an eyebrow. "What? Right here?"

Laxy nodded. "Yes, right here. Do it now."

Hari hesitated. He was not a show-off, but he was intrigued as to why Laxy should want him to dance. There must be some reason, and perhaps that would become clearer once he had started to dance.

Hari took a step forward. Then he took one to the side. Then he took a leap, landing in a crouch, like a spring ready to bounce back. The effect was electric. Not bothering even to put down their shopping bags, the crowds of people around Hari began to dance in step. They did everything that Hari did, and soon that entire side of the market, including the stall-keepers, were engaged in one great Bollywood dance routine. It was an astonishing sight.

After a while Hari stopped. Everything returned to normal and now that the crowds had thinned he was able to look about him for Laxy and Gav. He had lost sight of them while he was dancing, but he was sure that they would still be somewhere close by.

It was a few minutes before Hari saw the other two boys. They were coming towards him, each carrying a large bag.

"Come over here," Laxy whispered as he drew close to Hari.

Hari followed them to a closed doorway at the side of a shop. Checking that they were not being watched, Laxy opened the mouth of the bag he was carrying. "Look in there," he said.

Hari peered into the bag. Inside he saw a small radio, still in its packaging, a couple of penknives, a mobile phone, and a few other items that he could not quite make out.

"Gav's got a lot of stuff too," said Laxy.

"You can look if you like," said Gav, opening his bag for Hari's inspection. "It's all thanks to you."

Hari was puzzled. "What have I got to do with the things you bought?" he asked.

"Bought?" mocked Laxy. "We didn't buy these things. We took them."

Hari drew in his breath. "You ... you stole them?" he stuttered.

Laxy nodded. He seemed not in the least ashamed. In fact, he looked pleased with himself.

"We stole them from stalls while you

distracted everybody with your dancing. It worked perfectly. Nobody saw us helping ourselves – they were all too busy dancing."

"Yes," said Gav. "You helped us a lot. And we'll give you your share once we sell these on to Mr Banerjee. He'll be here any moment."

Hari struggled to control himself. He was an honest boy who would never dream of stealing anything – and here he was having helped these two thieves to get away with all sorts of expensive things. *I helped two thieves*, he thought in despair. *I helped them steal these things.*

Of course, he had not meant to help, and so nobody could really blame him for what happened. But Hari still felt terrible.

"I don't want anything," he protested. "If I had known you were going to do that, I would never have danced." He paused. "And I will never do it again."

Laxy grinned. It was an unpleasant sort of grin – not a friendly grin, but a threatening one.

"Oh yes, you will," he said quietly. "Because you're now part of our gang. You helped us, and if you don't do the same thing in future, then we'll let the police know that you were our helper."

Hari was about to protest about this, when Laxy suddenly pointed to a car that had drawn up nearby. "That's him," said Laxy. "That's Mr Banerjee here now."

CHAPTER SEVEN

The thieves learn a lesson

Mr Banerjee stepped out of the car. He was a thin man with eyes that darted to one side and then to another, as if he were looking for an escape. When he opened his mouth to greet Laxy and Gav, Hari saw that his teeth were sharp. They reminded him of a rat's teeth – teeth that could give you a nasty nip if you were not careful.

"So, boys," said Mr Banerjee. "What do you have for me this afternoon? Anything worth having?"

Laxy opened his bag to show the contents. "It's good stuff, Boss," he said. "And Gav's got some too."

Mr Banerjee peered into the bag. He smiled with satisfaction. "Not bad work," he said. "Put them in the car and I'll give you your money tomorrow."

Laxy took Gav's bag and put it, together with his own, in the back of Mr Banerjee's car. Mr Banerjee then glanced in Hari's direction. "And who is this?" he asked.

Laxy rubbed his hands together. Hari was his discovery, and he wanted to get the credit for finding him. "This is our new assistant," he said. "He's called Hari, and he distracts people."

Mr Banerjee frowned. "Distracts people?"

Laxy told Mr Banerjee what had happened. "He's a really amazing dancer, Boss. When he dances, everybody else starts to dance too. They can't help it."

It was clear that Mr Banerjee did not believe this for a moment. "I don't think so," he said.

Laxy turned to Hari. "Show Mr Banerjee, Hari."

Hari scowled. He wanted to have nothing further to do with these people. Laxy and Gav were thieves, and Mr Banerjee was the man to whom they sold their stolen property. And yet he remembered Laxy's threat. If he did not help them, he would be accused of stealing things and handed over to the police. He would try to tell the police what had really happened, but would they believe him? It would be his word against the word of two others – Laxy and Gav – and they might believe two boys rather than one.

Reluctantly, Hari began to dance. Mr Banerjee looked on with a strange expression on his face – one half way between disbelief and astonishment. Then, against his will, he began to dance alongside Hari, while Laxy and Gav joined in.

When Hari stopped dancing, they all stood still and looked at one another.

"Well, well," said Mr Banerjee. "That's a very rare talent. I see what you mean, Laxy. This young man will be a great help."

"Shall we show you how it works?" suggested Gav. "We could go back to the market with you, Mr Banerjee. Then you'll see just how easy it makes our job."

"A good idea," said Mr Banerjee, turning to Hari. "Welcome to the team, young man."

Hari looked about him. He could run off, but there was something threatening in the way that Laxy looked at him that put him off any idea of getting away. So, much against his will, he accompanied Mr Banerjee, Laxy and Gav back to the market. There were more people about

now, and the stalls were busy. Nobody paid any
attention to Hari and the two other boys, except
for Mr Banerjee, of course, who stood to the side
and prepared to watch.

"Dance!" hissed Laxy.

Hari hesitated.

"Remember what I
said," Laxy warned under
his breath. "Dance!"

Hari began to dance, and although it took
a few minutes before people began to notice
him, the effect of his dancing soon showed itself.
Customers from the stalls turned around and
began to join in, stall-holders left their customers
and started to dance among themselves. And
while all this was happening, Laxy and Gav set
about the business of stealing from the stalls.

When Hari saw what
was happening his heart
sank. He was being used by
these thieves and he felt
ashamed of himself. *No*, he
thought, *I can't let this happen, even if they have
threatened me.* And it was just at that moment
that a policeman, attracted by the noise of
hundreds of people dancing, appeared around the
corner.

This was Hari's chance.
Hari skipped across the road,
made his way towards the
policeman and danced in
front of him.

"There are thieves
stealing from the market,"

he said, his voice low. "Those two boys over there and that man standing watching."

The policeman looked in the direction of Laxy and Gav just as the two boys were in the act of stealing a radio. He gave a shout, and then blew hard on his police whistle.

What happened next all took place quickly. Hearing the whistle, the boys spun around, saw the policeman, and then began to run away as

fast they could. Mr Banerjee witnessed what was happening and ran too. For a moment Hari stopped dancing. He was unsure what to do, but he understood that if he did nothing, the thieves were likely to get away. But then he had an idea. If he could get enough people dancing in the street, the two thieves and Mr Banerjee would find their escape route blocked.

And so, that is what he did. Hari doubled his efforts and gave a great leap high in the air. Then he took several quick steps forward and made a turn. Next, he clapped his hands together, dropped to a crouch, and spun around one way and then the other. He used every dance step he could think of – and plenty more he had no idea he knew. And it worked. It worked far better than he had imagined.

All across the market, people began to dance, many of them moving as vigorously as Hari himself. Laxy and Gav were forced to stop in their tracks as they became surrounded by smiling, dancing people. The same fate befell Mr Banerjee, who suddenly found himself circled by lively, swaying ladies all trying to get him to dance with them. He brushed aside each

proffered hand, but no sooner had one hand been rejected than another would come forward. It was impossible for him to move, and with a snarl, his sharp teeth exposed but incapable of saving him, he realised that he was trapped.

At first, the policeman had been too astonished to do anything. But now he called for help on his radio, and within a minute or two other policemen had appeared on the scene. It was short work for them to arrest Laxy and Gav, along with Mr Banerjee.

By now, Hari had stopped dancing and the crowd had dispersed. He could have stayed to accept the thanks of the police and the market traders, but Hari was not that sort of boy. He did not need praise, and so he slipped away home, where his aunt and sister were waiting for him. His life had become rather exciting, he thought, and he wondered whether what would happen next would be as exciting as that day's events.

It would.

CHAPTER EIGHT

No admission

The next day, Hari told Mr Ram what had happened in the market. The old man listened, a smile crossing his face as he heard the story of Mr Banerjee and his young thieves.

"The police have been trying to catch those fellows for a long time," he said when Hari finished his tale. "They'll be pleased – and so will the market traders."

He stopped, and looked thoughtfully at Hari.

"You know, Hari," he said. "When you can do something really well, it's a pity not to use your talent."

Hari listened. He understood what Mr Ram meant, but how could he possibly use his gift of making people dance?

Mr Ram thought for a few moments before he picked up a newspaper from the table near his chair. "I don't suppose you've read the paper today?" he asked.

Hari shook his head.

Mr Ram pointed to a photo on the front page. A group of important-looking people were standing in a room. Their gaze was fixed on the camera, but none of them was smiling.

"These people," said Mr Ram, "are having a big meeting – right here in our city. Look at them.

Look at all the medals on that fellow's chest."

Hari looked and saw that several of the people were soldiers, and had very smart uniforms, complete with rows of medals.

"They must be very important to get all those medals," said Hari.

Mr Ram rolled his eyes. "Pah!" he snorted. "Who needs medals? These people are trying to sort out some trouble that's been going on up in the mountains. People have been fighting each other and it's all been very nasty. But will they get anywhere in these talks they're having?"

Mr Ram looked at Hari, as if waiting for an answer to his question. But Hari did not know, and so Mr Ram gave the answer himself. "They will not!" he said. "It's all hot air. They'll argue with one another for days. They'll fail to agree about anything. And then they'll go off and the fighting will start again. You mark my words, Hari – that's all that will happen."

Hari looked sad. He did not like people to fight. What was the point? If you fought, everybody simply ended up worse than before. Surely, he thought, it was far better to talk about what was bothering you and find a solution that way.

Mr Ram was staring at Hari. His eyes lit up as an idea came into his mind. Was it possible? Could it work?

"Listen to this, Hari," he began. "If the people in the photo could only be made to like one another, then perhaps things might get better."

Hari nodded. "But how could that happen?" he asked. "They're enemies, aren't they?"

Mr Ram shook his head. "You should never say that. Have you not heard the saying? People say that an enemy is simply somebody you haven't made friends with yet. Think about that, Hari."

Hari did, but he still could not see these important-looking people making friends with one another.

But Mr Ram could.

"I think we need to go there," he said.

"Where?" asked Hari. "Go where?"

Mr Ram looked thoughtful again as he tapped the front page of the paper with a finger. "It says here that their meeting is at the army base. We could go out there. I know where it is."

Hari frowned. "But won't there be guards?" he protested.

"There will be," said Mr Ram. "There'll be lots and lots of guards. These important people always surround themselves with plenty of guards."

"And even if they let us in," Hari went on, "what then? Do you think we could make them change their minds?"

Mr Ram laughed. "You think the answer to that is no." He chuckled. "But I think it's yes."

"But when would we go?" Hari asked.

"Now," said Mr Ram, rising to his feet. "I just need to find my outside shoes, and then we can be off."

"You haven't eaten your lunch," Hari said, pointing to the untouched tiffin box.

"Tiffin can wait," said Mr Ram. "There are more important things in this life than tiffin, Hari."

Mr Ram was right, of course, but then Hari remembered that he had made a special packet of sweets for him. He now took this from his bag and passed them across to the old man. Mr Ram's face lit up when he saw what the packet contained.

"Coconut *barfi*!" he exclaimed. "My favourite!"

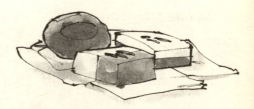

Hari smiled as Mr Ram took a square of the coconut sweet and popped it into his mouth.

"Delicious," pronounced Mr Ram. "You're a real star, Hari."

Hari looked down at the ground. He was a modest boy and it embarrassed him to be praised too much. But Mr Ram had said all he wanted to say about that, and now, licking the last of the pink coconut off his fingers, he led the boy out of his house and into the busy street outside. They would find a bus, he said, and this would take them close to the place where they wanted to be.

"And then?" asked Hari. "Then what do we do?"

"We'll see what happens," said Mr Ram. "That's often the best thing to do, you know, Hari – you see what happens."

*

There was a bus stop close to the gate of the army base, and it was here that Mr Ram and Hari alighted. Just as Hari had feared, there were soldiers on guard – at least ten of them, all standing to attention, all bedecked with weapons of one sort or another.

"They'll never let us in," said Hari, his heart sinking. "Nobody will be allowed in – unless they're important – which we aren't."

Mr Ram shook a finger at him. "You shouldn't say that, Hari," he scolded. "Everybody is important – even the youngest, smallest, weakest, poorest of us. We're all important."

"Yes, but ..."

"No buts, Hari," continued Mr Ram. "We shall simply go up to them and ask them to let us in."

Hari did not argue, but as they approached the guards, he felt his breath coming in short bursts. It was a familiar feeling – the feeling you get when you're about to do something really risky, something you know you should not be doing.

"Halt!" one of the soldiers shouted. "Where do you think you're going?"

Mr Ram was very polite. "Excuse me, Sir," he said. "But we were hoping to get inside in order to talk to the people at the big meeting."

The guard let out a snort. "You'd like to get in, would you?" he asked. "Half the country would like to get in, you know, but half the country can't. And nor can you."

Mr Ram looked at the other soldiers, but they were all smirking and nobody seemed prepared to do anything to help them. He bent down and whispered in Hari's ear.

"Start dancing," he said.

Hari was taken by surprise. "Right here?" he asked.

"Right here," said Mr Ram.

Hari took a deep breath. Then, with a snap of his fingers, he began to dance. He leaped up in the air, he ran a few

steps, skipped a few more, and then turned in a complete circle, all the while humming a catchy Bollywood tune. It was a splendid performance – one of his best.

Straight away, the mood changed. The senior guard, the one who had spoken to them earlier on, started to smile. Then he began to dance, as did all the other soldiers, all in one long line. It was a fine sight, with all the dancers in uniform, all keeping in step with one another like soldiers on parade.

Mr Ram tapped Hari on the shoulder. "Now's our chance," he said, pointing to the hotel at the end of the drive.

With all the soldiers caught up in their dance, each trying to do better than the soldier next to them, nobody noticed the old man and the boy as they slipped past the barriers. Nor did anybody pay much attention when they made their way up the steps outside the hotel.

"We're almost there," Mr Ram said, his voice low. "I think the meeting must be taking place in there."

He pointed to a large door on which a notice had been hung saying,

SECRET MEETING – NO ADMISSION.

"It says we can't go in," Hari pointed out.

He waited for Mr Ram to say something, but there was no reply. Mr Ram was not listening. He was far too excited to be worried about something as simple as a notice.

CHAPTER NINE

A very rowdy meeting

They stood for a moment in front of the closed door.

"Ready?" asked Mr Ram.

Hari was anxious. "But what are we going to do?"

Mr Ram repeated the question. "What are we going to do?" he said. "We're going to dance, Hari. Or, rather, *you're* going to dance."

And with that, Mr Ram pushed open the door and bundled Hari into the room beyond.

Hari gasped. They were now in an extremely large room – a ballroom – with a high, gold-painted ceiling. An immense table ran down the middle of the room, and at this table there sat about fifty important-looking people. Some of them were the people who had been in the newspaper photo – Hari and Mr Ram had not seen the others before.

The people at the table were all talking at once and paid no attention to the arrival of Mr

Ram and Hari. In fact, none of them even noticed them, but continued to shout at one another at the top of their voices.

"You've got it all wrong!" shouted one man in a uniform lined with generous lengths of gold braid.

"I've got it wrong?" shouted the man on the other side of the table. "No, you're the one who's got it wrong. You've always been wrong – always."

"I've never been wrong!" the first man

shouted back. "Unlike some people I could name – such as you!"

A few seats down, a tall woman in a red dress was shouting at an equally tall woman in a blue dress. "Don't you dare!" she yelled.

"Dare what?" retorted the blue dress.

"Dare say anything!" came the reply from the red dress.

"I'll say whatever I want to say," said the blue dress.

And at the end of the table, another row was in full swing. "You started the whole thing," cried a man in a black suit. "It's all your fault."

Opposite him, a man in a white suit shook his head vigorously. "I didn't start it," he protested. "You did."

"I didn't!"

"You did."

"Didn't."

"Did."

The man in the black suit shook his fist. "You shut up!" he shouted.

"No, *you* shut up," came the heated reply.

From half way down the table a voice protested, "You both shut up! We're trying to argue and it's very difficult to argue if other people are shouting."

Mr Ram glanced at Hari and shook his head sadly. "Would you just listen to these people?" he said. "This is no way for people to behave."

Hari agreed. He thought these people rather rude, and he very much doubted if they would ever reach any agreement.

"Time to dance," Mr Ram whispered.

Hari looked about him. He was shocked by the bad manners of the people in the room. If this was how adults tried to solve their differences, then it was no wonder that the world was so full of unsolved problems. If this was the way that people talked to one another, then was it any wonder that there was so much fighting and unhappiness in the world?

"Come on, Hari," urged Mr Ram. "Please dance."

Hari hesitated, but only for a moment. Then, singing his favourite Bollywood song, striving to make his voice heard over all the bickering, he danced his way across the room. Once he reached the table he paused. Should he or should he not? He decided that he should, and with one leap he was up on the table, dancing energetically all the

way down to the bottom
and then back up to the top.

A gasp rose from all
the people at the table.
Then, once their surprise
abated, they pushed their
chairs back and rose to
their feet. That led to

dancing – to a very major amount of spirited
dancing, some of it on the floor and some with
Hari on top of the table.

Mr Ram watched with sheer pleasure. "Show
them, Hari!" he muttered under his breath. "Show
them what dancing can do."

Soon everybody in the room was dancing
with the very people with whom, only a few
minutes ago, they had been fighting.

Red dress danced with blue dress. Black suit danced with white suit. People who had only a short time earlier been shouting at one another were now smiling as they offered their hands to their new dancing partners. Nobody was left out – and everyone looked friendly and cheerful.

Hari danced for a good half-hour. Then,

exhausted by the effort, he stopped, and one by one

the people at the meeting stopped too. They did

not go back to their old seats, though – they stayed

with one another, arms around shoulders, looking

as if they had been dear friends all their lives.

"Look," said Mr Ram. "These people are now

all friends."

There was a woman who had been in control
of the meeting, and she now banged a small
wooden hammer on the table to attract attention.

"Ladies and Gentlemen," she said. "I think we
are now all agreed on one thing at least – that it
makes no sense at all to fight with people."

There were nods of agreement. "Quite right,"
a man in uniform said. "Friends don't fight."

"They certainly don't," another man said. "They shake hands."

That was the signal for everybody to shake hands. There was no shouting now – just nods of agreement, along with smiles, and bursts of laughter.

"Look at that," said Mr Ram. "What a change!"

Hari nodded. He felt tired, but was very pleased that all these people would be going back to the mountains with an agreement that there would be no fighting. And if his dancing had helped to bring about that result, then he was pleased that he had been able to help.

"You see, Hari," Mr Ram whispered as they made their way out of the hall. "That gift you have is more powerful than hate. Hate is very weak, you know, when you meet it with kindness and friendship – and dancing is all about kindness and friendship, you know – that's what it is."

Hari had never thought of this before, but he realised that it was true.

"I think we should go back home," said Mr Ram. "I've just remembered something."

"What is it?" asked Hari.

"Your coconut *barfi*," said Mr Ram. "The packet is still there in my house. And there's still some left."

"Then you're right," said Hari. "That's a very good reason to go back."

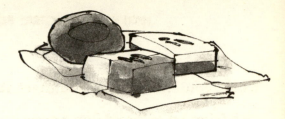

CHAPTER TEN

World peace now!

That is the story as I first heard it. The person who told it to me said he thought that there might be some more to it, but he was not sure. I thought no more of it, but a few months ago I heard what happened afterwards, and so I've added this final chapter.

A few weeks after that business in the hotel, long after everybody had gone off, word came down from the mountains that the long-standing disagreements up there had at last been settled. The friendships made in dance had lasted, and had brought everybody to their senses. So, rather than fighting with one another, people now worked out ways of making life easier for their former enemies. Not surprisingly, everybody was quite a bit happier.

And what about Hari and Mr Ram? Well, one day Mr Ram came to Hari with some very important news. The President of India had heard about what had happened at that meeting in the hotel and was very pleased with the result. He sent a message asking if Hari would care to go with him on an important tour he was about to undertake of foreign countries.

"You'll have to go, Hari," said Mr Ram. "This is a request from the President of India himself."

He paused. "And he's asked me too."

Hari could see that Mr Ram really wanted to do the trip, and that he would not go at all if Hari refused. So he said yes, and he was rewarded with a wide smile from Mr Ram.

A few days later, they were taken to the airport in a Government car to catch a plane to Delhi. There they met the President, and were soon flying in his official plane over the high mountains of the Himalayas. Hari had never been in a plane before that day, and he very much enjoyed looking out of the window at the snow-covered peaks of the great mountain range below.

They landed in Rome first, where the President had a tiny cup of coffee and a slice of pizza with the President of Italy. Afterwards, they all went to meet the Pope, who gave Hari a small packet of toffees and a sherbet fountain. When the President had finished talking to the Pope, Hari was asked whether he would care to show the Pope some Bollywood dancing.

Of course, not even the Pope could help himself from joining in, and soon Hari and the Pope were leading a long line of cardinals and bishops in a very colourful Bollywood routine.

Some of the cardinals had been arguing with one another before this, but now they stopped.

After Rome, they called in on London, where Hari was taken to visit the guard outside Buckingham Palace. Those guards usually stand quite still, but with Hari around that all changed. Soon the red-coated soldiers were dancing step by step alongside Hari, allowing him to try on their famous bear-skin headdresses. The Queen

saw all this from a window in the palace, but she did not mind too much. She liked her guards to have a good time, as there is nothing worse than being guarded by people who look miserable or discontented.

Then it was on to New York, where Hari danced at the United Nations HQ and brought several meetings to a very happy conclusion, getting old enemies to dance with one another. From there, they went on to Washington, where Hari succeeded in dancing his way past the police officers and Secret Service agents protecting the President. All these people danced with one another and felt very much better at the end of it all. Even the President danced, and later said that she had not had so much fun for months, if not for years.

At last they returned to India, and to their normal lives. But by now, Hari and Mr Ram had become famous, and had carried out various engagements at which Hari danced and brought people together. Mr Ram never charged a fee for these, but Hari insisted that he should have a share of the proceeds, and eventually he did. With his share, Mr Ram built himself a new dance studio where he could teach people how to dance, ably assisted by Hari.

But the biggest treat of all – at least from Hari's point of view – was that with the reward money the President of India had given him, he was able to bring his parents to live in the city. Not only that, but Mr Ram soon found them a job running the tea room attached to his dance studio. They did that very well, not only providing the customers with fine tea but with plates of sweets made by Hari. Even the aunt had a job to do. Mr Ram asked her to make special dancing clothes that they sold to the people coming for lessons. It kept her busy and enabled her to buy a new sewing machine. She was very content.

Hari's parents were most interested to hear about their son's success as a dancer.

"Wherever did you learn to dance so well?" Hari's mother asked.

"By watching other people," said Hari.

"That's a good way of learning anything," Hari's father said.

Hari and Amala were pleased that they had been joined by their parents. Life had worked out well for them, just as it had worked out well for all those people whom Hari got to dance.

Dance was something special, Hari and his family realised – it brought out things within you – deep things – that could change the way you looked at the world. It made you smile. It made you laugh.

It made you understand that there were other people in the world apart from yourself, and that these people could be your friends. Dance did all of that.

"I'm very happy," Hari said to his sister a few days after his parents arrived. "I'm happy that our parents are here. I'm happy that Mr Ram has a new studio. I'm happy about everything, I suppose."

"So am I," said his sister.

Hari looked thoughtful. "I think I'm going to make a fresh plate of coconut *barfi*," he said.

"Good idea," said his sister.

From somewhere in the background, there came the sound of Mr Ram clearing his throat.

"Don't worry," said Hari. "There'll always be enough for you, Mr Ram."

"Oh, I know that," Mr Ram called out, licking his lips. "In fact, I think I may have two pieces."

Hari smiled. "Or even three," he said.

"Why don't you dance yourself?"

When Hari realises he has a special talent for dancing it changes his life – and the lives of lots of other people too. When Hari dances, other people can't help but join in. And dancing together makes everyone happy!

You can enjoy Hari's magic gift too. Here are Hari's Top Tips for places to dance ...

1. "The great cameras started to film"

If you are an actor you can do a marvellous, energetic dance on a stage or film set – or you can make-believe and dance just like a film star!

2. "Hari went out into the yard"

You can dance in your yard or back garden – perhaps while a dog snoozes under a tree. Don't worry if you don't have any music. You can sing or hum or whistle, or simply dance to the music in your head.

3. "People came to his studio from far and wide"

If you are lucky enough to know someone who has a dance studio where you can take lessons, then it is lovely to learn new dances with a barre and mirrors and a springy wooden dance floor.

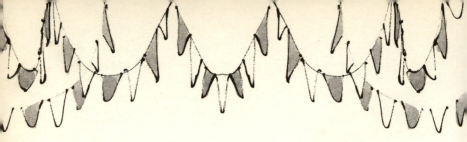

4. "A concert in the street"

You and your friends might like to put on a special concert for all your neighbours – perhaps in the park or a street where there's no traffic. You can send out invitations and everyone can dance together in the open air.

5. "The people at the big meeting"

If you find yourself in a very important but dull meeting where everyone is arguing and shouting then perhaps you can help them solve their problems. You could distract them – but only with a major amount of spirited dancing. (Why not ask an adult to try this at their work – and report back to you!)

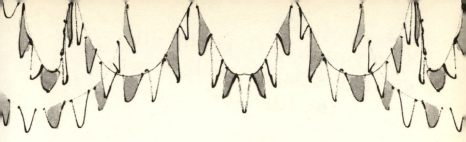

6. "The guard outside Buckingham Palace"

This is a very difficult challenge! But there's nothing to stop you doing your best dancing outside the palace, or anywhere else. Like Hari, you can dance anywhere and everywhere, and however you want, but remember ...

WARNING! It's best not to dance ...

- In the shower – you might slip and fall.

- In the kitchen with sharp knives – it's dangerous.

- When you're crossing the road – be safe and wait till you're on the pavement to dance!

Can you help Hari and all his dancers dance their way to the film set?

Start

Finish

COCONUT BARFI

Make top-class coconut barfi just like Hari with this easy-to-follow recipe.

You will need

- 400g tin of sweet condensed milk
- 500g of desiccated coconut soaked in a bit of milk for 30 minutes and then drained (or you can grate two fresh coconuts!)
- A few strands of saffron to make the barfi yellow
- A teaspoon of cardamom powder
- A metal baking sheet or plate (with slightly raised edges)
- An adult's help!

Method

1. Grease the tray or plate very lightly with butter.

2. Put the condensed milk and coconut in a pan and mix together.

3. Turn on the heat and cook. Stir ALL the time until the mixture starts to come away from the sides of the pan. This only takes a few minutes.

4. Add the saffron and the cardamom if you have them.

5. Stir well and turn the heat off.

6. Pour onto the tray or plate and smooth out with your fingers or a spatula. Don't make it too thin – you want nice chunks of barfi.

7. Leave to cool completely.

8. Cut into squares and lift out carefully with a spatula or knife.

9. Eat and enjoy!

"Oh, Hari, you must be one of the best sweet-makers in all India."

ALEXANDER McCALL SMITH

is one of the world's best-loved authors. He is particularly famous for his *No. 1 Ladies' Detective Agency* books, which have sold over 20 million copies worldwide. Alexander has written more than 30 books for children and has won many awards, including the British Book Awards Author of the Year Award in 2004, a CBE for services to literature in 2007 and, in 2017, the National Arts Club (of America) Medal of Honor for Achievement in Literature. Alexander lives in Edinburgh, a city he loves to explore in his stories. He would love to take dancing lessons from Hari, as he says he has a lot to learn when it comes to dancing.

"McCall Smith believes that the small stuff in life matters" *SCOTSMAN*

"McCall Smith's blend of gentle humor and insights into human nature is irresistible" *PUBLISHERS WEEKLY*

"The books, like their author, have charm. You cannot overstate the power of this – it's the missing ingredient in contemporary fiction" *GUARDIAN*

SAM USHER spent most of his childhood reading, drawing and forgetting to do school work. He still likes to spend his time messing around with ink, watercolour and washing-up liquid. Sam's first book – *Can You See Sassoon?* – was longlisted for the Greenaway Medal. Sam lives in London and, when he isn't drawing, he enjoys playing fiendishly difficult Chopin on the piano. Sam says, "I had just visited India when I first drew Hari – plus I am partial to a jaunty leg in my illustrations! – which made it a joy to work on this story."

About ... HARI

Alexander McCall Smith says, "I had tremendous fun writing about Hari, and setting his story in India, a country that I find fascinating. Hari not only makes excellent Indian sweets, but he is also a great fan of Bollywood dancing. Indeed, who *doesn't* like Bollywood dancing? Hari discovers that he is what you might call an infectious dancer – and, effectively, it turns out that he dances for World Peace. Such is the power of dance to change our lives!"